Princess Pip's
Vacation

SALLY PRUE

Illustrated by Korky Paul

dingles & company

COMMUNITY LIBRARY NETWORK
AT POST FALLS
821 N SPOKANE STREET
POST FALLS, ID 83854

First published in the United States of America in 2008 by
dingles & company
P.O. Box 508
Sea Girt, New Jersey 08750

First Printing

Website: www.dingles.com
E-mail: info@dingles.com

Library of Congress Catalog Card Number
2007906299

ISBN
978-1-59646-908-2 (library binding)
978-1-59646-909-9 (paperback)

Princess Pip's Vacation
Text © Sally Prue, 2007
This U.S. edition of *Princess Pip's Vacation*, originally published in
English in 2007 as *Princess Pip's Holiday*, is published by arrangement
with Oxford University Press.

The moral rights of the author have been asserted.
Database right Oxford University Press (maker).

Printed in China

Ready to Go

Everyone in Princess Pip's castle was very busy. The King was polishing his money, the Queen was choosing sun hats, and all the maids were running around with piles of clothes.

"Can I take Dobbin on vacation?"
asked Princess Pip.

"I'm afraid there won't be room for a
pony on the coach," said the Queen.

"Oh," said Princess Pip. "Can
Amanda and Bert come, then?"

"There's no room for snakes," said the King, "not even pet ones."

Princess Pip scowled. "This vacation is going to be BORING," she said.

They went on vacation in their best gold coach.

"Wave to all the people, dear," said the Queen.

Princess Pip folded her arms. "I'm on vacation," she said. "Are we nearly there yet?"

"We won't be there for a long time," said the Queen firmly.

It *did* take a long time to get to the seaside. The coach got very hot, and Princess Pip didn't feel very well.

"Here we are, at last!" said the King happily.

"But it's a castle!" said Princess Pip. "Just like home. It's BORING!"

2
Just Like Home

There was a girl waiting by the
castle door.

"This is Daisy," said the Queen.
"She's going to take care of you, Pip."

Daisy showed Princess Pip her room.
"I don't want a four-poster bed!" said
Princess Pip. "That's just like home!"

"You can sleep on my straw mattress,
then," said Daisy. "I'll have the bed."
"Oh, all right," said Princess Pip.

That evening there was a banquet, and it went on for hours.

"More sprouts?" asked the King happily.

"This is BORING," said Princess Pip.

"Nonsense, dear," said the Queen. "It can't be boring. We're on vacation!"

"I WANT TO GO HOME!" said
Princess Pip, the next day. She had
been walking around the castle walls
all morning, and she hadn't found
anything to do.

"But we're having a wonderful time,"
said the Queen, from her sun chair.

"Just look at the way my money shines in the sun," said the King. "Wonderful!"

"But it's BORING!" said Princess Pip.

"Why don't you go and talk to Daisy?" suggested the Queen.

Princess Pip stomped off.

"That does it," she said to Daisy. "I WANT TO GO HOME!"

3

The Road Home

"If you stayed here a little longer, you might start liking the seaside," said Daisy.

But Princess Pip wasn't listening. She was putting all her important things in her suitcase.

"I think we'll have to take some things out," said Daisy.

Daisy found them both backpacks,
and they set out for home.

Princess Pip and Daisy went across
the drawbridge and along the road.

It was very hot.

"Let's have a nice, cool snack,"
said Daisy.

So they got some fish sticks from
a stand.

"These aren't bad," admitted
Princess Pip.

"They taste best by the seaside," said
Daisy. "I'll show you where the fish
come from, if you like."

They went down some stone steps to a
place where the sea swished backward
and forward, and the ground looked as
if it was made of gold.

"Look in these pools," said Daisy.

The fish were hard to catch.

"You could take your stockings off," said Daisy, "and use them for nets."

It was nice without shoes and stockings on. It was even nicer once Princess Pip had taken off her coat and crown.

The fish looked unhappy being caught, so Princess Pip let them go.

"It's not too bad here," said Princess Pip, at last. "I want to stay here all the time."

"Let's build a sandcastle, then," said Daisy.

"A sand HOUSE," said Princess Pip.

It was hard work, but they built a
huge house, with a moat all around.

Soon the sea came in and filled
the moat.

"That's just right," said Princess Pip.
"Make it stop coming in now, Daisy."

But the sea kept on coming in...

... and soon it had washed their house FLAT.

"We built our house too close to the sea," said Daisy, sadly.

"STUPID SEA!" shouted Princess Pip. "STUPID SEASIDE! I WANT TO GO HOME!"

4

Riding the Dragon

Princess Pip and Daisy put on their shoes and picked up their backpacks.

"I'm tired," said Princess Pip, very soon. "I want to ride Dobbin. Are we nearly home, yet?"

"Why don't you ride one of the horses on that merry-go-round?" suggested Daisy.

"Oh, no," said Princess Pip. "I'm going to ride that dragon."

The dragon went very fast, and there was lots of exciting music – but then it all stopped. Everyone got off.

"But...we're still here!" said Princess
Pip, crossly, as she got off, too.

"At least it wasn't boring," said Daisy.

"I WANT TO GO HOME!" shouted
Princess Pip.

"At least it was fun," said Daisy.
"Everything is fun here because it's a
FUN-fair."

Princess Pip sniffed. "What's fun about it?" she asked.

"I'll show you," said Daisy.

They went down the roller coaster.

Then they went UP and UP and...
DOWN again.

"AARRRRGH!" yelled Princess Pip
and Daisy.

"Let's go on it again," said
Princess Pip.

"Tomorrow, perhaps," said Daisy,
who had become very pale.

"BUT I WANT..." began Princess Pip.

"Hello!" said a voice.

It was the King. The Queen was with him.

"Where's Princess Pip?" the King asked Daisy.

"Here!" said Princess Pip.

The King and the Queen stared at her.

"You can't be Pip!" the Queen gasped. "You're all dirty, and you have no stockings!"

"But I am!" said Princess Pip, and
put on her crown to prove it. "Look!
It's me, and I've found a place where
the ground is made of gold!
Come and see."

Daisy and Princess Pip showed them the beach.

"Good heavens!" said the King. "How wonderful! It's just the color of money."

"What a perfect place for my sun chair," said the Queen.

The beach was a perfect place for
picnics and games, and races, too.
Everyone loved it.

Then one day the King said: "What
a pity we have to go home tomorrow."

Princess Pip scowled, and she said...

About the author

Our family always had
trouble choosing somewhere
to go on vacation. My mom
needed there to be a gas
stove, my dad needed
a garage for the car, and
my brother needed
somewhere where they
made fishing boats.

I needed SAND.

I expect lots of families have the
same sorts of problems. Even when
they are very, very rich!